S0-AFB-368

Polar Bears

ABDO Publishing Company

A Buddy Book

by
Julie Murray

VISIT US AT

www.abdopub.com

Published by Buddy Books, an imprint of ABDO Publishing Company, 4940 Viking Drive, Suite 622, Edina, Minnesota 55435.

Printed in the United States.

Edited by: Christy DeVillier
Contributing Editors: Matt Ray, Michael P. Goecke
Graphic Design: Maria Hosley
Image Research: Deborah Coldiron
Photographs: Corbis, Corel, Minden Pictures, Photodisc

Library of Congress Cataloging-in-Publication Data

Murray, Julie, 1969-
Polar bears/Julie Murray.
p. cm. — (Animal kingdom. Set II)
Contents: Bears — Polar bears — Their bodies — Coat and color — Where they live — Food — Cubs — Traveling bears — Saving polar bears.
ISBN 1-59197-332-5
1. Polar bear—Juvenile literature. [1. Polar bear. 2. Bears.] I. Title. II. Series: Murray, Julie, 1969- . Animal kingdom. Set II.

QL737.C27M895 2003
599.786—dc21

2002038560

Contents

Bears

Bears have been around for millions of years. Today, bears are the largest meat-eating, land animals. Three kinds of bears live in North America. They are the American black bear, the brown bear, and the polar bear.

Black bear
Brown bear
Polar bear

Polar bears are mammals.

Baby mammals drink their mother's milk.

Bears are **mammals**. Mammals are born alive instead of hatching from eggs. They use lungs to breathe air. Female mammals make milk in their bodies to feed their young. Most mammals have hair or fur. Giraffes, tigers, seals, and people are mammals, too.

Polar Bears

Polar bears are the largest bears in the world. They live where it is very cold.

The polar bear's Latin name means "sea bear." Polar bears are good swimmers. They can swim 50 miles (80 km) without resting.

Polar bears are good at running, too. They can run as fast as 25 miles (40 km) per hour.

Polar bears are good swimmers.

What They Look Like

Polar bears are big and strong. Males grow to become about four feet (one m) tall. Standing on two legs, male adults are about 10 feet (3 m) tall. They weigh about 1,100 pounds (499 kg). Female polar bears are smaller.

Sometimes, polar bears stand on two legs.

Polar bears have small ears and a short tail. Their big paws are 12 inches (30 cm) across. They have special pads on the bottom of their feet. These pads help polar bears walk on ice without slipping.

Special foot pads help polar bears walk on ice.

The polar bear's coat is very thick. There are two layers of fur. The outside fur is colorless. The inside fur is white. The polar bear's fur draws heat from the sun. It helps the bear stay warm.

Polar bears spend as much time on ice as they do on land.

Polar bears have black skin. Under the skin is fat, or **blubber**. This thick layer of blubber also helps polar bears stay warm.

Where They Live

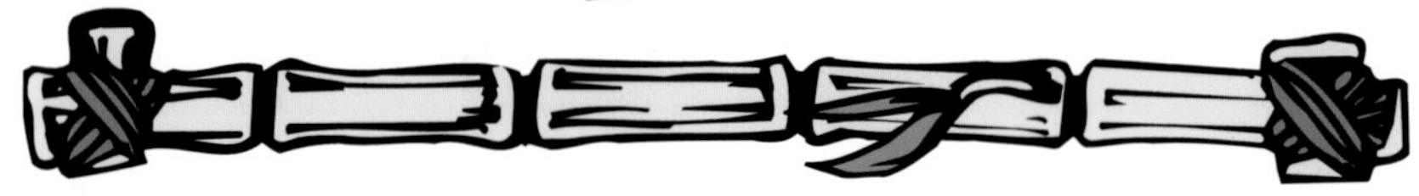

Polar bears live in the Arctic. The Arctic is near the North Pole. Polar bears live in Alaska, Canada, Greenland, Norway, and Russia.

Polar bears mostly live near the coast. They live on ice and **tundra**. The tundra is land that stays mostly frozen.

On very cold days, a polar bear may dig a snow cave. The bear goes inside and curls into a tight ball.

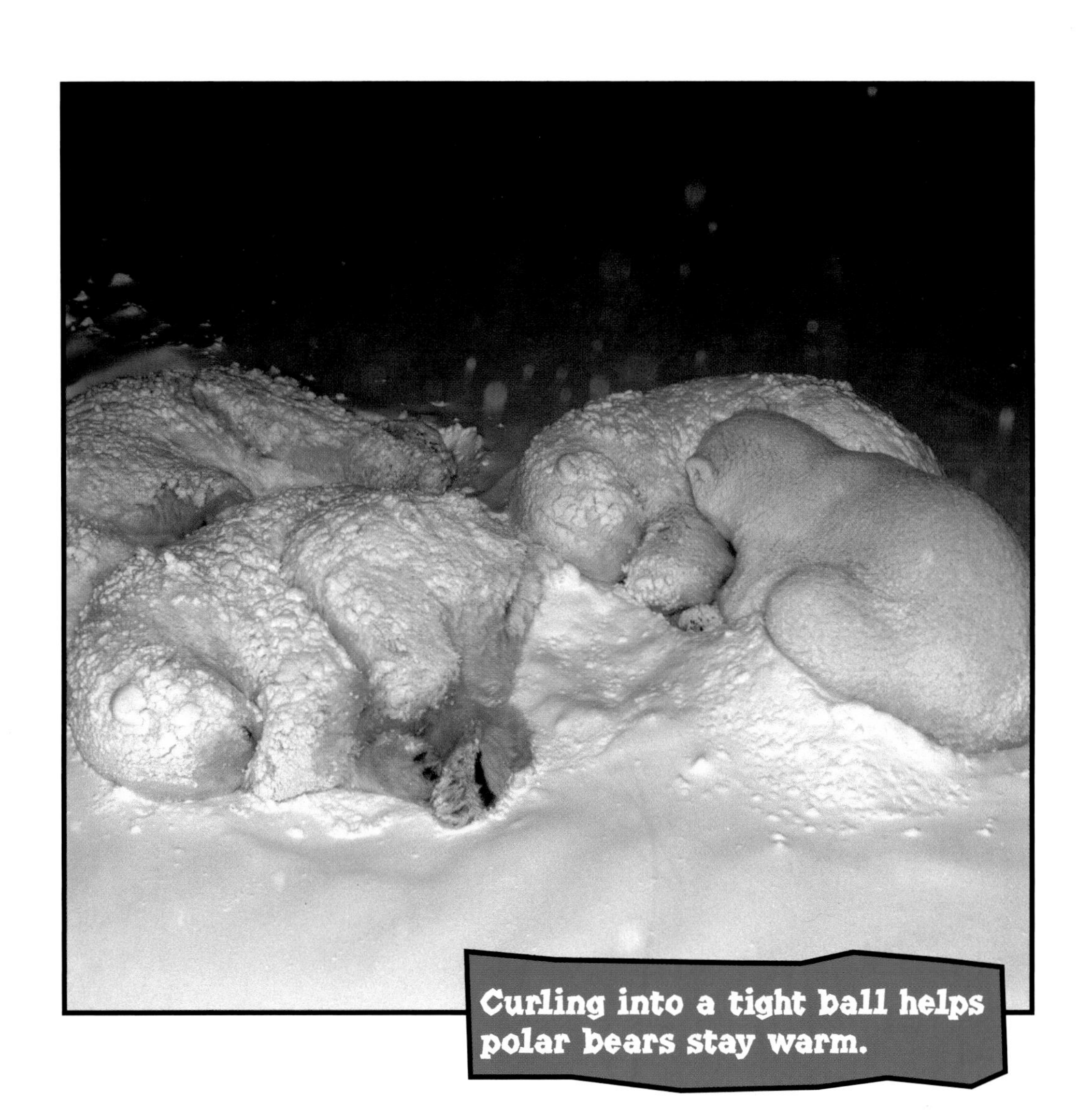

Curling into a tight ball helps polar bears stay warm.

Eating And Hunting

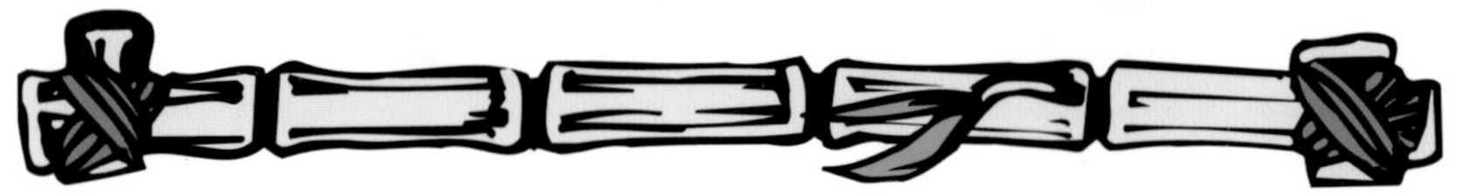

Polar bears can eat 150 pounds (68 kg) of food at one time. They eat seals, walruses, fish, and other animals. Polar bears also eat plants. They enjoy berries, seaweed, and grass.

Polar bears have a keen sense of smell. This helps them find seals and other **prey**. Polar bears often hunt ringed seals. Sometimes, polar bears catch seals while they are asleep.

Seals are the polar bear's favorite prey.

Some polar bears wait for seals by holes in the ice. This is where swimming seals come up for air. When a seal comes up, a polar bear can catch it.

Migrating

Polar bears travel far each year. This is called **migrating**. Polar bears migrate to find food. Some polar bears migrate hundreds of miles each year.

Arctic waters have big chunks of ice called **ice floes**. Migrating polar bears sometimes ride these ice floes. They may ride ice floes for many miles.

Polar bears migrate many miles each year.

Polar Bear Capital

Churchill is a town in Manitoba, Canada. It is on the coast of Hudson Bay. Some people call Churchill the polar bear capital of the world.

Polar bears **migrate** through Churchill twice each year. People visit Churchill to watch the migrating bears.

Bear Cubs

Baby polar bears are called cubs. Female polar bears commonly have two cubs at one time. She gives birth in a hidden place called a **den**. Cubs are commonly born in December or January.

Newborn cubs weigh less than two pounds (one kg). They cannot hear or see. The hairless cubs stay near their warm mother. They drink her milk.

The mother and cubs leave their **den** in the spring. By this time, the cubs weigh about 25 pounds (11 kg). They can run and play. They stay with their mother for two or three years. Polar bears can live as long as 30 years.

Bear cubs learn to swim and catch their own prey.

Important Words

blubber fat underneath the skin of polar bears, walruses, and other animals.

den a hiding place where animals raise their babies.

ice floes ice chunks that float in the ocean.

mammal most living things that belong to this special group have hair, give birth to live babies, and make milk to feed their babies.

migrate to move from one place to another when the seasons change.

prey an animal that is food for another animal.

tundra flat land with no trees in the far North.

Web Sites

To learn more about polar bears, visit ABDO Publishing Company on the World Wide Web. Web sites about polar bears are featured on our Book Links page. These links are routinely monitored and updated to provide the most current information available.

www.abdopub.com

Index